About the story

The Yoruba live mainly on the coast of West Africa, especially in Nigeria, where they are the largest ethnic group. The Yoruba language is spoken by over 10 million people in the southwest of Nigeria.

Their historic kingdom dominated West Africa up to the 18th century. In Yoruba folklore, goddesses rule the pantheon of superior beings. Thus, Ile is goddess of earth, Yemoja is goddess of water and her daughter Aje is goddess of the Niger River, from which Nigeria takes its name.

Versions of this traditional Yoruba tale can be found in a number of collections, including *West African Folktales*, William Barker, (Harrap, London, 1917); *Africa: Myths and Legends*, Alice Werner (Harrap, London, 1933); *Fourteen Hundred Cowrie: Traditional Stories of the Yoruba*, Abayomi Fuja (Oxford University Press, New York, 1964); *African Folktales*, Roger D. Abrahams (Pantheon Books, New York, 1983); Jan Knappert, *African Mythology* (Diamond Books, London, 1995)

How to pronounce the names

Yemoya – *Yem-oy-ah*   Aje – *Eye-yeh*   Oduduwa – *O-doo-doo-wah*

For Chloe ~ **J.R.**

The Coming of Night copyright © Frances Lincoln Limited 1999
Text copyright © James Riordan 1999
Illustrations copyright © Jenny Stow 1999

First published in the United States in 1999 by
The Millbrook Press,
2 Old New Milford Rd
Brookfield, CT. 06804

First published in Great Britain in 1999 by
Frances Lincoln Limited, 4 Torriano Mews
Torriano Avenue, London NW5 2RZ

Library of Congress Cataloging-in-Publication Data
Riordan, James, 1936-
   The coming of Night : a Yoruba tale from West Africa / James Riordan ; illustrated by Jenny Stow.
     p. cm.
   Summary: When the daughter of the river goddess Yemoya goes to the Land of Shining Day to marry a handsome earth chief, her longing for the cool darkness of her former home causes Night to be brought to the world.
   ISBN 0-7613-1358-3 (lib. bdg.)
   [1. Yoruba (African people)—Folklore. 2. Folklore—Africa, West. 3. Night—Folklore.] I. Stow, Jenny, ill. II. Title.
   PZ8.1.R4495Co 1999
   398.2'089'96333—dc21   98-24261
                          CIP
                          AC

The Coming of Night

A Yoruba Tale from
West Africa

By **James Riordan**

Illustrated by **Jenny Stow**

The Millbrook Press • Brookfield, Connecticut

Long ago, when the earth was new,
it was forever day.

No moon, no stars, no night-hunting
owls and leopards.

No dawn to tell people when to rise;
no dusk to tell them when to sleep.

The land was bathed in bright sunshine
all the time.

One day the great river goddess, Yemoya,
sent her daughter, Aje, to marry a handsome
earth chief, Oduduwa. Aje left her shady home
in the river's depths and went to live in the
Land of Shining Day.

At first Aje was happy in her new home, and she loved her husband dearly. But after a while she began to tire of the unrelenting sun. She told her husband, "This sunlight hurts my eyes. How I long for the cool shadows of my mother's home beneath the waves! How I wish that Night would come!"

Oduduwa was surprised.
"What is Night?" he asked.
"Night," said Aje wistfully,
"is a cool veil that curtains
the day's warm bed. It is the
gentle sigh that calms a restless
heart. It is the welcome rest
that refreshes a weary soul."
"Where is Night?" asked
Oduduwa.
"Only in my mother's
realm beneath the waves
can Night be found," said Aje.

At once the young chief went down to the river to talk
to Yemoya's messengers, Crocodile and Hippopotamus.
  "Go to Yemoya," he said, "and ask her for Night.
Say it will make her daughter happy."

Crocodile and Hippopotamus dived into the watery depths.
They swam through the coral reefs, the gloomy caves,
and dark grottoes. Finally, they came to a glittering palace.

Yemoya herself
came out to greet them.
    Bowing low before her,
they explained their mission:
Her daughter longed for the shades of Night.
    Straight away, the goddess filled a sack
full of Night for them to take back to earth.
    "But heed my warning," Yemoya told them.
"Do not open the sack until you reach my
daughter. Only she can control the spirits of Night."

Swimming through the swirling waters, Crocodile and Hippopotamus bore the sack between them until they reached dry land. Once on the bank, they stopped to rest and dry themselves in the sun's warm rays.

All at once, they heard the strangest noises coming from the sack. They had never heard the sounds of Night before, and they made them quake with fear.

"Let's throw the sack back into the river," said Hippopotamus.

"No, let's open it up and see what is inside," said Crocodile.

With that, he undid the knot with his sharp teeth and pulled open the heavy sack.

Whooosh!

Out rushed the night insects: midges,
moths, gnats, and spiders.

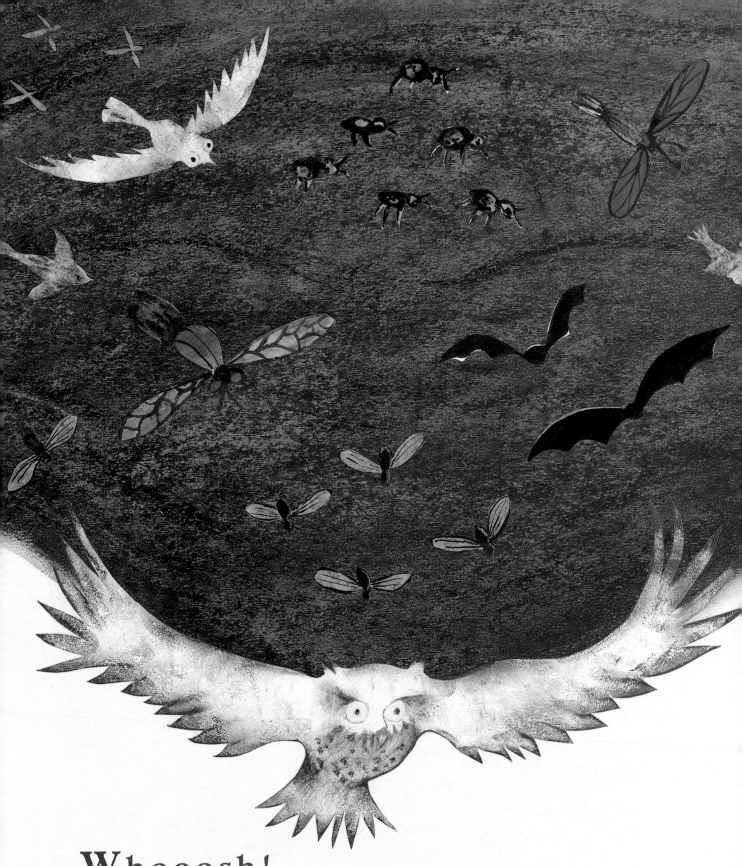

Whoooosh!
Out rushed the night birds: owls, jars, and nightingales.

Whooosh!
Out rushed the night animals:
leopards, lions, bats, and bullfrogs.

All these night creatures terrified Crocodile and Hippopotamus.
They dived deep into the muddy waters, then reappeared
in mid-river with just their eyes and noses above the swell.

Aje was waiting on the bank, sheltering beneath a leafy palm. The moment she saw the swarms of insects, flocks of birds, and herds of animals, she uttered a low cry.

All at once, the spirits of Night grew calm, and a hush
descended on the land. The gentle hum of insects spread
throughout the bush. Twinkling stars gazed down from
a dark blue sky, and moonbeams trod a silvery path across
the waves. Owls hovered above woodland glades, and leopards'
eyes gleamed behind the trees. The cool air grew fragrant
with the scent of Night; a murmuring breeze rustled the
forest leaves.

Aje smiled. Now she knew she would find peace in her
husband's land, and she fell into a deep sleep.

When she awoke, Aje gave her new home special gifts.

To the brightest star shining in the sky, she said,
"You shall be Morning Star, announcing the birth
of each new day."

To the cockerel crowing on the wattle fence, she said,
"You shall be guardian of Night, warning us when
day is breaking."

To the birds chirruping all about her, she said,
"You shall sing most sweetly
at dawn, waking people with
your song."

And ever since then,
Morning Star, the cockerel,
and the birds all announce
the coming of each new day.
But only after the restful
sleep of Night.